MW01075628

About the Author

Rebekah is a social psychologist, university lecturer, and mindset coach. Her professional and personal experiences keep her focused on the intricacies of the human condition and the need to balance competing demands. In her spare time, she enjoys reading, writing, and the outdoors.

Nobility

Rebekah Wanic

Nobility

Vanguard Press

VANGUARD PAPERBACK

© Copyright 2024
Rebekah Wanic

The right of Rebekah Wanic to be identified as author of
this work has been asserted by her in accordance with the
Copyright, Designs and Patents Act 1988.

All Rights Reserved

No reproduction, copy or transmission of this publication
may be made without written permission.
No paragraph of this publication may be reproduced,
copied or transmitted save with the written permission of the publisher, or in
accordance with the provisions
of the Copyright Act 1956 (as amended).

Any person who commits any unauthorized act in relation to this publication
may be liable to criminal prosecution and civil claims for damages.

A CIP catalogue record for this title is available from the British Library.

ISBN 978-1-83794-293-0

This is a work of fiction. Names, characters, businesses, places, events and
incidents are either the products of the author's imagination or used in a
fictitious manner. Any resemblance to actual persons, living or dead, or actual
events is purely coincidental.

Vanguard Press is an imprint of
Pegasus Elliot Mackenzie Publishers Ltd.
www.pegasuspublishers.com

First Published in 2024

Vanguard Press
Sheraton House Castle Park
Cambridge England

Printed & Bound in Great Britain

Dedication

To everyone who has shared a part of their story with me

Chapter 1

"Well, what am I supposed to do? I'll call you back."
He slammed the receiver down.

"What was that about, honey?"

"I can't." He dismissed her with his hand, turning toward his study.

Shutting the door, he revisited the conversation. *Your father is in a coma and his systems are failing. Absent a DNR, the medical decision-making is yours. We are calling to see what course of action you would like us to take.* The nurse had droned something to that effect, making him wonder if she was reading from a script. He wondered how many times in her career she'd had to make this kind of call, hoping it was a lot. If not, her detached manner struck him as cruel.

What should I do? His thoughts returned to the urge he'd felt to kill the man just a few months back. Back when everything had finally come to light, through the very public arrest and trial. *And he's still causing me problems. Can't even* die *on his own. What an asshole. I'll let him die.*

But. His thoughts caught as he felt a twinge, maybe guilt? *Shouldn't that be his decision? SOB that he is, shouldn't he still get to have the final say over what happens? What if he wakes up? Will they be able to get his opinion then? Will he even be capable of giving consent, of signing a DNR?* It was times like this when Rupert wished that he was a lawyer.

"I'd hate to call Ken to ask." He recalled his neighborhood pal who was now a prominent attorney. "He'd just end up asking *me* a bunch of questions."

Rupert had been avoiding contact with most of his friends from back home lately, anyone who would have known his father. He just couldn't bear the questions, the awkward conversations, and the wondering. Wondering from their side, and from his. *Did something happen to you?* He knew what would be on their minds. *Did you sense anything?* Rupert would wonder about them in return. It was better not to know, just better not to talk at all.

"Damn. How can this be happening?" He put his hands on his head, letting them slowly pull down over his face. But his skulk toward self-pity was interrupted by a soft knock on the door.

"Honey." He heard her hesitant voice as the door cracked open. "I, I just wanted to check if you were OK. You sounded upset. Can I get you anything?" She peered in cautiously, almost as if using the door to shield herself.

God, why is she such a mouse? He felt the sneer form with his thoughts. *I hate her for being meek, but I made her that way. Maybe that's why I hate her, she makes me see what an asshole I am, and I punish her for it. I am an asshole, I should be nicer.*

"No, I'm fine," he said aloud, catching his scorn and adjusting his tone. "The First is in a coma and somehow I'm the medical decision-maker." He sighed.

Rupert referred to his father as "The First" these days. In full, he was Rupert Nathaniel James I, making Rupert himself the II. Such a pretentious name, he had always hated it. All their names were pretentious – Rupert II, Sebastian, his brother, and Greta, his sister. His father had picked them, a message of what he wanted for his children. "A child grows into their name, and I have chosen aristocratically," that was The First's position. Rupert always felt that these names were also a rebuke against his mother, Mary and, although he'd pointed out that Mary was the name of several queens and the mother of Jesus, his father viewed it as plain.

Growing up, to his father's dismay, Rupert's friends called him "RJ" and to Rupert, the First had been "Dad." He just couldn't bring himself to call him that any more. The "Dad" he knew was a lie, an illusion. He never existed, or if he had, he couldn't exist any more. Not after everything Rupert learned at the trial.

His response to her inquiry was more curt than intended, his attempt to control his tone unsuccessful, and she began her retreat. "Oh honey, how awful," she said with concern, already slinking back. "If you want to talk, let me know. I'll leave you alone, just know I'm here. I'm gonna get the kids to bed." He heard her softly shut the door.

I should really be nicer, he thought again as she left. *There's nothing wrong with her. She's kind, a great mother, she takes care of me. I just can't stand her* presence *sometimes.* He worked to unclench his jaw. Rupert's feelings were driven by more than just her niceness highlighting his character flaws. She was too nice, too good. She lacked that edge, that piece that made people interesting. Vanilla was the pejorative people threw around these days. And she was just that, a basic vanilla. Light blonde hair, pale white skin, preferring to dress in pastels. Shit, her name was even simple: Jill.

"Fuck it!" He grabbed the phone, hearing the bath water running. This would give him at least forty-five minutes as she dealt with the two kids in the tub before wrapping them in soft pajamas and under their covers, so he made his call.

"Hi, sexy!" The voice on the other end cooed, greedily asking, "How was your day?" She always asked this with a touch of hope, as if she had forgotten what was going on in his life. His days were not those about which one could feel hopeful, but he loved this about her. She'd never stop waiting for him to have an optimistic answer.

"Shit, it was shit," he intoned, his distress plain. "You won't believe the phone call I just got." As he spoke, the relief washed over him, his muscles relaxing without the need for effort, knowing she would listen and question and offer advice without patronizing. He loved her.

"Tell me. What's going on?" She turned from playful to concerned, readying herself for his pain, his confusion, his anxiety, his hatred and to help him process.

"That asshole's in a coma, health failing. The hospital called to let me know that they might need to make some decisions and..." he paused. "And, I'm the lucky fuck with the decision-making authority."

"Oh wow, what a load." She exhaled the words, a sign she understood the position he found himself in.

This is why I talk to her and not to Jill, he thought. She was insightful in a way unlike anyone he knew. He always felt that half of what he wanted was in her awareness before he shared a word. *She's easy,* he'd often thought. Easy to love, easy to make love to, easy to talk with, easy in every way. Well, every way except one: their situation wasn't easy.

"What are you thinking?" she began with a gentle probe in her usual manner. "Are you upset because he's dying or upset that you have a hard decision to make? Maybe both?"

Every angle, he thought, *she sees every angle.*

"To be honest, I'm not upset about either of those things, not really." Although, he knew that if he thought about it a bit more, both would show up as part of what bothered him. "The thing I'm most concerned about is not knowing what he wants… and making the wrong decision."

It took a bit longer to get the last part out, because he didn't want to admit it. Why should he continue to worry about what his father would want? He wanted to just write him off, to hate him, just let him go. But he couldn't.

"And that bothers you, that you still care?" she asked, reading his thoughts.

"God, you see right through me, dove. Yes, why *should* I care? He doesn't deserve it."

"Well, maybe he does, maybe he doesn't. We can return to that later. I'm just wondering why it bothers *you* when you find evidence that you might be a good person. Continuing to care about someone you loved for many years is normal. You can't just shut it off."

"Maybe," he said slowly, trying to process and compose his thoughts at the same time. "I guess I'm angry that he created this situation. You know how much he didn't want that prison transfer. I wonder if he just stopped taking his meds."

"Probably," she agreed. "In that case though, you know what decision he'd make, would want you to make. That should make you feel better."

"But, what if he changed his mind?"

"When, while he was in the coma?" He knew she was smirking at the thought of someone unconscious changing their mind. She was quick-witted and loved to banter. Someone who didn't know her as well might think that she was insensitive to the difficult questions she asked or her interjection of humor when things were serious. He loved this, even though he was often the target of her challenges.

"No, I mean when he wakes up. What if he changes his mind when he wakes up? It's possible, you know. Lots of times people who get a second chance think differently."

"Sure, he could, but it's probably unlikely. He's got nothing like a new lease on life if he wakes up. He'd be back in prison, ready for the transfer he doesn't want. Facing the rest of his life in prison. He's not looking at anything changing for the better." She paused, "Plus, he's old and unwell."

The more he listened, the more he realized that he was being selfish. He wasn't sure if he'd wanted a new crisis to distract him, to make it easier to ignore the real feelings he needed to process. This decision wasn't really difficult at all, he was brooding over other things.

"What does the rest of your family think? Have you talked with your mom or Greta?"

"Mom, no, I can't bother her with this. She hates him even more now. He's hurt her so much, and I'm sure it seems like it never ends these days. She's had to deal with everyone back home since this story broke. All the looks, the questions. And all that on the heels of Sebastian. She doesn't need any more. I'll give Greta and my aunt a call tomorrow, see what they think. But you're right, I know what I should do."

"Anyway, enough about me," he transitioned, changing his tone to mirror hers when she'd answered. "What about you? How was your day? And make sure to tell me what you're wearing – I want to accurately undress you as you talk." He smiled, thinking of how she'd be rolling her eyes at him for this last comment.

"Tomorrow, it's late. I'll fill you in tomorrow. You're still coming over, right? Usual time?"

He hung up a few minutes later, in time to get a little work done before Jill returned from upstairs.

"Honey," she said softly as she half-opened the door with a light knock. "I'm going to pour myself a drink and head up to read in bed. Would you like me to pour you a scotch before I go?"

He got up to meet her at the door, opening it fully to let her in and pulled her to his chest, smelling the soap from the bath on her skin. She turned into his hug with warmth. "I'm really sorry, hon." She kissed his chest and looked up. "I know you've been dealing with a lot. I can take the kids to my mother's for a few days if you need some space. I'm not trying to desert you, just want to help you so you can deal with this. It's been a rough couple of years for the James family."

He took her cheeks in his hands, turned her face up toward his and kissed her softly. "Jill, thank you. I've been a bear, and you are nothing but wonderful. Can I come upstairs with you? I could use some company tonight."

She kissed him greedily, knowing what he wanted. "Sure, I'll meet you up there with our drinks."

* * *

Later, Rupert lay awake, listening to the slow, soft breathing beside him. He turned on his side to face her, observing her as she lay on her back, watching the way her breasts lightly rose as she inhaled. He leaned in to kiss her, revisiting his decision to be nicer. He gently moved the hair that fell over her chest to kiss the space between her breasts, his hand grazing her nipple. Laying her blonde locks to the side, he traced from her shoulder to her throat, running his fingers along her clavicle and then down her sternum to her navel.

She stirred at his touch and he felt himself harden, but it was late and he wanted to get some sleep. He knew she'd want to continue, and it would be his turn to please. "She's good to me," he'd reminded himself earlier, setting down his scotch on the nightstand as she'd moved to straddle his lap. He'd tried to reach up, to touch her once his hands were free, but she pushed him away, holding his hands above his head as he lay on his back. "Just relax, pay attention to how it feels," she'd instructed, adjusting her position and pace to help him.

"She's good to me... but I'm bored." He turned away from her, settling into his pillow. She knew what to do, they'd had years of practice, but it was all pastel. "Vanilla," he'd scoffed, even as she'd cradled next to him, drifting off when he'd finished. *I guess I could change it, ask for a change, but she'll get upset. I'm not in the mood.* He closed his eyes. Tomorrow, she'd ask him how it was and he'd lie to her like always.

Chapter 2

Because he traveled frequently for work, Rupert and Jill had decided that she needed the opportunity to travel too, to get out and explore, and to get some time without the kids. She would usually plan a trip with some of the other stay-at-home moms in the neighborhood, or the few friends from college that she still kept in touch with, four or five times a year. Jill liked her free time, but she was usually anxious to get back, so hers were mostly weekend trips, with an occasional larger vacation mixed in.

This weekend, she was in Reno with her two "college besties" as she put it. He'd always cringed when she used this ridiculous expression, hating how it made her sound like she was trying to be young and fun, using someone else's phrase like an imposter. "Poser" was the popular pejorative for someone like that when he was younger. It reminded him of those old women dying their hair with streaks of blue or pink after teenagers had started doing it a few years ago. *Don't they know it looks ridiculous? Originality is not copying, it's inventing your own thing*, he'd assert, mostly to the audience in his head.

Because he hated playing the games the children had at home and was not one to participate in traditional activities like hide-and-seek, Rupert would usually fill time by taking the kids somewhere during the days he was responsible for them. He was never upset or annoyed that he had to watch them. He loved his kids and enjoyed spending time with them, but he needed to control the environment so that it included things that he enjoyed as well.

This time, he decided that they would visit the zoo. "Yes! I love the zoo!" squealed Isabella. "Can we see the monkeys?"

"No, no monkeys," pouted Chad. "I want to see the lion!"

"Kids, no fighting or pouting. We can see both. And so many more. *I* really want to see the leopard," he said, leaning down to tickle his son lightly, helping the pout evaporate.

Isabella was two years older, and bossy. She liked to get her way, but Chad had learned from Jill that pouting would overrule bossy in the hierarchy of the household, at least when the roost was ruled by Queen Vanilla.

"You let him pout." Rupert would scold her. "I don't want a son who whines and pouts. Can we teach him a better response?"

"Sure, you can do it when you're here with him all day," Jill replied. She was never biting, but the only time she would *almost* get an edge was when he tried to instruct her on parenting. That was her domain, and he could readily admit, she was good at it. He knew he should keep quiet about it, but he'd comment nonetheless. The allowance made him feel like she was coddling the boy or worse, that she wanted to keep him dependent and weak. He'd grow up to be one of those ridiculous clichés, a man with mommy issues.

"Come on, kids, let's get to it! Put on your jackets and get in the car. Doors are open, so climb on in."

He grabbed the last of his things, packing some snacks, wipes, and other child-trip essentials into his backpack. He buckled the kids into their seats and drove the twenty minutes to the zoo. "Remember," he instructed on the way over, "no running off. There will be no Icees if I have to be chasing after the two of you."

"Yes, Daddy!" they chirped in unison.

They really are good kids, Rupert thought. *I'm a lucky man. I should be more appreciative of the work that Jill has done. Occasional pouting or not, they* are *well-behaved*. He would think such things often, but the time to share them with Jill never seemed to materialize.

After parking, he unbuckled and lifted the kids out of the car. "Wait here while I grab the snacks," he said.

"Eww, why did you bring snacks, Daddy?" Isabella turned up her nose. "They always get hot and melt."

"How do you know I brought something that will melt?" he asked mischievously. He knew she wanted to buy a snack at the zoo. He would of course give in, but the teasing made things more fun. "I bet you can't guess what I have."

"What, Daddy?" asked Chad. "Is it gummies?"

"No, no gummies. Try again."

"Granola?"

"Nope, not granola. Try again."

This back-and-forth went on as they walked toward the entrance until the kids were running out of snack items to suggest. "Give up?" he asked, as they neared the gate, their silence indicating that they were stumped.

"Yes, Daddy. What?" Isabella asked with all the exasperation a child of seven could muster.

"It's eel," he said, drawing out the word to make it sound longer. "Delicious eel. Just like a Twizzler, only more thick, slimy, and black."

"Eww!" both kids squealed. "No, Daddy!" said Chad with a whine. "I don't like eel."

"How would you know? You've never tried it, son." Rupert enjoyed these games immensely. The level of emotion with which the kids responded. Their tendency to believe what he said, to take him at his word until he gave them a signal that he was joking, it was part of the magic of parenting. Witnessing, and perhaps exploiting, their childish innocence and trustworthy nature.

"It's slimy, that's gross," he stated.

"I'm not eating it either," Isabella asserted.

"I guess you two will go hungry then." He feigned disappointment. "I really thought you'd like it. Well, more for me I guess." He shrugged, then turned to them with a smile. "Haha! I fooled you." He watched as their faces transformed from frowns to grins, waiting for him to say what he had really packed. "I really brought ice cream!"

"Daddy, how could you!" Isabella said as they all laughed. "It will melt for sure. I told you!"

He loved it when they got excitedly silly and laughed gleefully. The genuineness of their giggles made him feel warm, one of the few things that made him feel truly happy. That, and the time he spent with Flora. But, now wasn't the time to think about that. Now was the time to focus on the children, to make sure they had a good day.

"Well, if you don't like eel or melted ice cream, I guess we'll have to buy something. But, no snacks until we've seen at least ten different animals." He'd create concrete games to keep the kids occupied. "And no rushing to just see the first ten. And they have to be different types." He caught himself as he almost said species. "All the snakes count as just one of the ten." He tried to quickly make the rules, based on the loopholes he would have found when he was younger. He laughed to himself, thinking how he'd have run to the reptile hut, with about thirty different snakes in close proximity, in order to get the snack in a hurry.

Making up games was something his dad would do, too. He'd invent contests, along with prizes, to keep the three kids, Rupert and his younger brother and sister, occupied whenever they had a long drive. The family had a small sedan growing up, so all three had to sit next to each other in the back seat, packed in like sardines.

Suddenly, Rupert was reminded of the time when he was young, and his dad took them on a drive around the neighborhood to look at Christmas lights. His mother had stayed at home, so Rupert was allowed to sit in the front, giving each child their own window for optimal viewing. "I've got a dollar for the person who spots the most snowmen," his dad had announced as they began the drive. In those days, a dollar seemed like a big prize.

Poised at his window as the snow crunched under the wheels, Rupert began shouting, "There! I see one!" and "There's another!" as they rolled down the road.

"I don't see any," Greta said, sounding puzzled.

"I'm not seeing them either, son." His father queried. "How are you spotting them so quickly?"

"He's making it up," Sebastian chimed in with his characteristic whine. "They're not there. I don't see any. He's lying."

"Rupert," his father adopted a stern tone. "Are you cheating? You know that cheating is not right."

"No, I'm not cheating," he remembered protesting. "I'm not! I saw them all. There are lots of snowmen. You're not looking in the right place is all. Look at the windows too. There are decorations."

"Oh, so you *are* cheating," his father was displeased. "You knew what I meant. A snowman means *made out of snow*." He made sure to emphasize each word. "We'll just have to start over. Only snowmen made out of snow count. I shouldn't have to say it."

Rupert sunk into his seat, crushed by this rebuke. He'd anticipated that perhaps his father would reward him for his perceptiveness, his ingenuity, but instead, he was disappointed in him. Dejected, Rupert dropped out of the game and his sister and brother ended in a tie, each getting their own dollar.

When they got home, his father asked Rupert to stay back in the car. "You know, son," he'd scolded, "creativity can be a good thing, but you always want to stretch the rules. Be careful with your cleverness and tendency to deceive. They may help you get away with things, but that doesn't make it right."

God, he thought, coming back to the present. *I can't believe him. How dare he say those things to me when he was living such a lie!* Rupert was angry that he'd felt so upset that night. *How dare he, the hypocrite!*

"Daddy!" Isabella shouted and he came out of his reverie.

"Yes dear, I'm sorry. I was thinking about something else." They were at the gate, so he pulled out their passes and swiped them to activate the turnstiles. As they walked through, he looked to the right. A store was conveniently placed at the entrance, with stuffed animals, candy, and other goodies attractive to the child's eye positioned invitingly in the windows. He avoided that minefield skillfully by asking "Who sees the peacock?" This caused them to look past the store toward the main walkway, where a peacock was often strutting. There was no peacock there today.

Jeez, there I go again, he thought. *Saying I see something that's not there. The First would be so disappointed.* He felt his lips curl in spite. *Stop, Rupert,* he chided. *Focus on the kids.*

"What's first?" he asked, turning his attention back where it belonged. He anticipated hearing both "monkey" and "lion," which he did. "Okay, kiddos, if we walk this way, we will get to both in no time."

"And after ten animals, we get a snack," Isabella stated, her tone reminding him not to forget.

"Yes, I remember what I said, sweetie. Let's try to focus on why we're here though. To see the animals."

He felt like he was being curt, less playful than he was earlier. *Well, I probably am,* he thought. *I just can't get over the memory. I had completely forgotten about that lecture he gave me. What an asshole.* He was fighting back a strong desire to confront his father, but what good would it do? He was startled back to the present as he almost ran into someone who had stopped walking right in his path.

"Oh, excuse me," he started to say as she turned around. His voice caught with recognition. "Flora!"

he exclaimed, instinctually leaning in to give her a loving hug.

"Rupert, my word!" she said, hugging him back. "What a funny place to bump into you. Who're ya here with?" she asked, attempting to peer around him.

"This is Isabella, and this is Chad," he said, presenting and introducing the kids who were behind his legs in turn. "We're here for a daddy day. Jill's out of town."

"Well hello, Isabella; hello, Chad," Flora replied pleasantly, extending her hand to shake theirs with fake formality. "I'm here with my sister and my niece. They're visiting this weekend." She pointed to two people a little ahead, his head nodding as he remembered. "What's up? You seem a little distracted."

She always knows, he thought. *And really, I would love to talk with her about it right now. All this shit that just came up. She'd help me see it in a way that would make it less upsetting.*

"Tell you Monday," he whispered, knowing that he needed to keep his focus on the kids.

"Sure thing, love," she said naturally. He wouldn't have noticed but Isabella caught the last word and looked up. Noticing her mistake for the same reason, Flora mouthed, "Sorry."

He shrugged, but ended the conversation abruptly with a very unfeeling, "Well, great to see you," before turning and swiftly walking the other way with a wave.

"Who's that, Daddy?"

He cringed as she asked the question that he knew was coming. The one that would cause him to lie. "Oh, just a friend." He hoped that would be enough.

"She's pretty," Isabella stated the truth. "And, she likes you."

He cringed again. "Of course she does, sweetie. Your daddy's a nice guy." Why he said it, and in that stupid tone, he didn't know. It made him feel worse. A nice guy? Fuck, he was lying to her now and the family more generally with his ongoing affair.

Shit, what a great trip this is turning into, he thought, mentally blaming his foul mood on his father. *Move on, refocus, get the kids refocused,* he told himself.

"Kids, look what I see!" he said, pointing at the sign for the primate section. "Monkeys straight ahead! Let's go!"

His excitement was exaggerated because he wanted to get their attention back on the animals, to move on to something else. He didn't want to be forced to lie to them any more or field any more questions about Flora. Plus, he wanted to fill their heads with other things so they would forget about her. The last thing he needed was for Isabella to say something to Jill about meeting the pretty woman at the zoo who likes Daddy. He'd be forced to lie even more.

***

A few hours later, as he drove home after what turned into a great trip, the kids nodded off from a long day of walking, excitement, and sweets. It gave him time to revisit what he had recalled earlier.

I just don't understand it, he thought. *How could he be so two-faced?* But really what bothered him was, *How could he be so* right*?*

And he was right. Rupert's cleverness, and his tendency to break the rules, had helped make him highly successful, but these characteristics had also put him in *this* situation. A situation where, if he really probed deep into it, he was no different from his father, the man over whom he wanted to feel morally superior. He was lying to his family just like The First had lied to theirs.

"But," he tried hard to sustain the illusion that his transgressions were different, "I don't lie to them like *that*. I don't lecture my children like *that*. And, I don't punish them for things that aren't actually wrong. I was being clever, not deceptive with the snowmen. I wonder, was he so sensitive about *my* behavior because he was really upset about his own?" The parallels were disconcerting.

But, he renewed the thought that the behavior he was lying about was nowhere near as bad as the behavior that his father had kept hidden for all those years. "His *lies* were worse; his behavior was *worse*. It was criminal."

Rupert had struggled to understand his father's actions, wondering how a *father* could have done what he did. He'd never hurt anyone directly, at least nothing had come up in court, but harm to others occurred nonetheless.

"We may be similar, but I'm not *that* bad," Rupert tried to convince himself. "And, I'm not that hypocritical. I'm not *that* hypocritical." He sighed.

Chapter 3

The news about Sebastian's death had come two years earlier and was a shock to everyone. Rupert wasn't quite sure if it was more shocking or less shocking than the revelations about his father, or which was more tragic. But in reality, a comparison between the two events wasn't even appropriate.

It had been his birthday, Sebastian's 30th, and he was supposed to be meeting their mother for dinner at their childhood home where she still resided after forty-five years. She and The First were no longer living there together. He had moved out about five years earlier, shortly after retiring, but they had not divorced. The explanation given was that he "needed space." More realistically, he just couldn't stand to be in the house with her all the time now that he didn't have work to escape to. He was used to having more freedom.

To Mary, it was insulting. She boiled at the thought that he'd left her alone in that house, trotting off to work. Depending on her staying behind to keep the household going: take care of the kids, wash his clothes, cook his meals, host his parties. All that was done in *his* service, and when he'd had the opportunity to provide her with some companionship as they grew old, he wanted nothing to do with her. She'd outlived her usefulness to him, she supposed.

Of course, in hindsight, he *needed* the space. It would have been much harder for him to continue doing what he'd done if she was around to see him. His work computer and travel schedule had made it easy to hide it before he'd retired. But once those were no longer options to keep his images hidden, he'd sought more privacy, and a room, even his own room, in their shared house, wouldn't suffice. She'd be too likely to come in, wanting to clean or bother him when the door was closed. It wasn't viable, too many chances to get caught.

She knew nothing of what he was doing, of course. If she had, her decisions would have been different, but one can only base decisions on what they know. In hindsight, her insistence that they not get divorced would haunt her. "I don't want to deal with all of that," she'd told him at the time. "I will make it miserable for you if you try. Just get an apartment and move out."

Mary and The First had stopped talking after that, using Sebastian or Greta as go-betweens, both of whom still lived close by. Rupert was spared a similar fate because he'd moved away after college. It was smart to get out, to start anew. He was even more thankful for his decision to leave the area after the events of the past few years played out.

On that night, Mary had made a wonderful dinner, including all the things that Sebastian loved.

She'd labored over bacon-wrapped dates, a tart apple and cranberry salad, and seasoned pot roast with buttered red potatoes topped off with peach cobbler for dessert. She'd always made sure that the children felt special and cared for, attention to detail was her gift. She was good like that, remembering the favorites of each one.

Rupert always felt that she had been a wonderful mother and a wonderful wife. *She's just like Jill,* he'd thought in comparison on more than one occasion. Both paid careful attention to making their children feel special. But, of course, he couldn't be sure of the extent to which she was similar to Jill as a wife. But, from what he had seen, she'd treated his father well.

Because he wasn't there, Rupert had learned the details from Greta after the fact and subsequent conversations with his mother had filled in the rest. Sebastian was supposed to arrive at six but he was late, so unlike him, especially when he had plans with their mother. He'd always been her favorite, the baby, and he, a cliché with mommy issues, took pains to make sure that he didn't upset her. He knew that punctuality was important to her, especially when she was hosting a meal. She would time things just so, making it clear that the time you were supposed to arrive was the time you should arrive. This would ensure that each item in each course could be served at the precise moment it was ready.

After fifteen minutes, their mother called him to inquire about his tardiness. He didn't pick up, and after an hour, she drove to his apartment to investigate. It was only a five-minute drive, lengthened by growing anxiety. Mary had always worried about him more than the others. He'd been an emotional and moody child, growing into an emotional and moody adult with a penchant for indulgence in drugs and alcohol. The few other times Sebastian had stood their mother up were induced by overdoses or excessive partying, so she felt compelled to make the house call.

Knocking on the door to no answer, Mary let herself in, scanning the room quickly but seeing nothing that gave her pause. His place looked neat and tidy, none of the disarray of the past, with empty gin and vodka bottles on the floor or pipes and tar stains on the coffee table. "Sebastian?" she called as she walked inside. "Are you here, dear? It's Mom, I'm worried. You're late for your dinner."

She'd walked through the living room into the bedroom and screamed. Sebastian's body hung limp from the light fixture above. She'd dialed Greta, uttered only, "Come help, at Sebastian's" and fainted.

Greta arrived just a few minutes later, as she'd been on her way to share the birthday dessert, found two cold bodies and called 911. The paramedics were able to revive their mother, but she needed treatment for the bump on her head where she'd connected with the door frame and then the floor, and for shock. There was no treatment to revive Sebastian.

"Rupert," Greta said when he'd picked up the phone, simultaneous with his uttering, "I already sent a birthday text." He'd assumed she was calling with her usual reminder.

"No need," she said flatly. "He's dead. And that asshole almost killed Mom too." Her anger bubbled through her words as she explained "the party."

"Where's Mom now?"

"In the hospital still. She'll probably stay a couple of days. I don't really want her out soon. I've gotta go over tomorrow and clean up the birthday dinner. You know she'll lose it again if she sees the table set when she gets back."

"She's probably going to need to stay with you for a bit, I'd imagine," he offered, thankful that he lived so far away.

"Yes, asshole, of course, she will. Thanks for stating the obvious." He wouldn't get upset or defensive in return; he knew her anger was justified.

"And Dad?" he asked. "Does he know what happened?"

"Not yet. I figured you could tell him."

"Greta, why me?" Rupert whined. "You and he get along better. I don't know any of the details."

"Rupert, fuck you. You have removed yourself as much as you can from helping with this family. Yes, I could have made a choice to move away too, but it's different for daughters. Anyway, please, can you just call him? He can call me to talk later but right now, I need to break down. I can't be strong any more; I need to process."

"Sure, sis, of course. I'm sorry. You're right. Me being selfish. Yes, I'll call him, and let him know. Do you think I should tell him about Mom too?"

"You can, but what difference would it make? He's not going to go see her and I doubt she would want him to. I'll call you tomorrow, and start figuring out plans for the funeral and everything."

They said goodbye, leaving him to call his father with the news. The call was short; neither up for sharing his emotions. "Is your mother OK?" he asked.

"No, Dad," Rupert replied aggressively, his turn to displace some anger. "She hasn't been OK for years. But then, you should know that. She's resilient, but I'm not sure she's going to recover this time."

"Son, you don't get to lecture me." His father's retort was equally aggressive. "You don't know my life; you don't know our relationship. Your loyalty to your mother is admirable, but she's not a saint." Rupert could feel the sneer. "Relationships ebb and flow, some work, some don't. We all make choices and deal with the consequences. But, I *will not* let you tell me which choices I should have made. You think it would have been better if I'd stayed there and been miserable myself?"

"Now is not really the time, Dad, but thanks for the life lesson in selfishness. Call Greta tomorrow if you need more information." He hung up, tired.

As always, Jill was there when he got off the phone to listen were he so inclined to talk, but he wasn't so she just poured him a scotch. They sipped their drinks in silence, she going back to her reading after learning what had happened, leaving him alone with his thoughts. Later that night, she had comforted him in bed.

That was the beginning of the end of his relationship with his father. Rupert couldn't bring himself to talk to him at the funeral and the next time they had a conversation, it was after he had been arrested and was awaiting trial in jail. The visit was awkward, both for the setting and the topic.

Rupert forced out the questions: "Dad, I have to ask you, did anything ever happen with Sebastian? Is that the reason he was the way he was?"

Instantly furious, The First spat back, "How fucking dare you make such a sick accusation! You know that I loved all of you and would never hurt you. Of course, I never did anything to him, I've never done anything to anyone." He'd turned away, readying himself to leave the metal table.

"Dad, please." Rupert felt sick at his tone as he begged his father to stay. But he wanted some answers. The First stayed seated but turned to Rupert with a glare. "You have done something; you have hurt people. You've done things that harm children. Anyway, I needed to ask because it's been on my mind."

"I didn't harm him. I would never do that. I loved you kids with all my heart."

"Then how could you do all *this*?" Rupert said through clenched teeth.

"Because I never thought I would get caught."

"What? That's not what I mean. Why did you *do* this? How could you—you be interested in looking at *that*? Why?" Rupert wasn't sure why, but he wanted to know. What was it that was wrong with his father? What would drive a person who says that he loves his children to do this to other people's children? It was all so wrong, so incomprehensible.

His father looked down and sighed. "Son, you know, I don't have an answer for you. Everyone is flawed, everyone hides things from the world. Everyone does things that they know are wrong. We all make mistakes and we don't always have an explanation for them."

"Really, that's your answer?" Rupert's blood pressure rose. "People make *mistakes*? Mistakes! Fuck, you're saying that you are no different from everyone else? And you really believe that? Sure, we're all flawed, of course, no one is perfect. But we're not all flawed like *you*. Some sins, they are worse, they are worse than others, you have to know that. We may all have done things that are wrong, but not like this. Not like this."

We're not all the same, Rupert assured himself as he watched his father disappear behind the solid door.

I'm not like him. I can't be. He sat for a bit, finding it hard to lift his weight from the chair.

Chapter 4

Sandwiched in the middle of all of this James family drama was Rupert and Jill's anniversary. It was their 10th, and according to the etiquette guides, the traditional gift was tin or aluminum.

"Apparently, it's supposed to represent the durability and flexibility of the union." Jill read the online entry aloud.

Rupert scoffed, "Seriously, Jill? Aluminum?"

"Yes, that's what it says here. Why, what's so wrong with that?"

"Well, first of all, it's cheap. But more importantly, it's not in fact *durable*. Think about a soda can or tin foil. They are weak, they lose their shape with only a little pressure. That's not an image I want associated with my love."

She smiled so widely at his words that he felt guilty. He was in love, in love with one woman, maybe two, but the second was totally clueless about the first. Her innocence and love for him were all part of that vanilla aspect that got on his last nerve.

"What image do you want, honey?" she asked him with anticipation.

"I don't know, Jill, maybe titanium? Or crystal?" he offered with a smile and a shrug. "You know I love etched crystal. But gifts are silly. I just want to spend time together."

She smiled widely again, and he felt less guilty because his words were true. He didn't want any gifts, they had too much *stuff* accumulated already.

"Well then, let's go out to dinner somewhere really nice. No gifts… but maybe I can buy a new dress?" She clapped and folded her hands together underneath her chin, like a child. He laughed at her joke.

"Of course. Please, get a new dress. I'd love that." He leaned over to kiss her cheek. "I gotta run. I need to be in the office for a few hours this morning, but I'll be back early afternoon. I'll take care of the restaurant; you take care of the dress. See you later." They parted with a quick kiss.

She seemed so happy, his guilt returning with the thought as he pulled out of the driveway. *I am happy with her too… sometimes, I guess.* He directed his car toward Flora's apartment.

On the way over, he walked himself through his relationship with Jill. *Why did we get married? What did I want from this relationship? What* do *I want now?*

He and Jill had met in college. They were both in first-semester calculus, and she was hopeless. He'd offered her help with the course because he found her attractive. Wasn't that the play in college? He made sure that she was able to pass the course, but she continued to struggle with most of her classes for the rest of their time there. Luckily, he was academically gifted and able to do the work for both his courses and hers, earning them solid GPAs at graduation.

Jill was appreciative, in and out of the bedroom, and to the casual observer, they made a good pair. She was an attractive blonde and he was a handsome, intelligent engineer. After completing his undergraduate degree, Rupert enrolled in an MBA program, finished in a year and a half (he was only doing one set of classes) and graduated with several high-paying job offers. She'd worked in an office for a bit during that time, but a month before graduation, he'd proposed. She'd quit the job to focus on planning the wedding as he wrapped up his coursework.

Six months later, they were married in a small ceremony with mostly family and a few friends. After the wedding, they honeymooned in Europe, sampling cities where his Italian and her French would get them by. Before the taste of the cake frosting was gone, his unease with Jill's vanilla flavoring began to show.

He remembered when they were in Paris, visiting the Louvre. He'd been excited to see the hidden gems, wanting to look at all the paintings that most people didn't know were there or paid little attention to. She was only interested in those that were most popular. His nose turned up as he thought about her inability to pick her *own* favorite. *Don't let it bother you,* he tried to tell himself. *Everyone has their own tastes. Yes,* he countered himself, *but your tastes should be* your own, *not something you like because someone else tells you you should.*

As their trip continued, this same scenario played itself out time and again. She was taking in Europe based on what she'd heard was interesting or beautiful, but he sensed that she wasn't judging it for herself. He found himself hating her a little for it, this lack of originality. At the time, he wrote it off as post-wedding commitment issues. *I'm probably just looking for things to pick at because I feel nervous about the finality of this whole marriage thing.* He tried to convince himself, to set it aside.

But it never went away. The kernel of hatred was watered frequently. Every time he sensed that Jill made decisions based on consensus, which was nearly every decision she made, he felt the pang. He was profoundly disappointed in her lack of originality. He wondered sometimes if things might have been different had they not had the kids, had she been able to get out and make a life of her own. But then again, he told himself, she probably wouldn't have done that since having kids was what she thought she was supposed to do, it was the next step in her picturesque life.

He smirked somewhat meanly as he thought about Isabella and Chad. *Isn't the boy supposed to be older in an ideal world?* he wondered. When he thought about Jill and the life she had, it always made his thoughts drift to his mother. Did *she* feel trapped, did *she* feel stifled by the expectations that came with being a wife and mother? He had a sense that his desire for originality was inherited from his mother, that she could have been and wanted to be so much more.

But who was he to judge? And how dare he project his values on them. Perhaps these women felt that they were more, had more than him. I mean, they did spend their lives helping others to grow, caring and nurturing. Wasn't that in some way nobler than his endeavors in originality out there in the "real" world?

But really, how interesting can you be when you spend all day in the home? Conversations with a seven and five-year-old are not the most intellectually stimulating, and for the most part, neither is daytime TV. He'd met her neighborhood friends too, and they were not going to introduce Jill to philosophical debate anytime soon. From his perspective, Jill's life was simple, she was simple. Vanilla.

Why was he with her then? It was a legitimate question, but he knew the answer. He was with her *because* she was simple, because it was easy. Not in the way that being with Flora was easy, easy in the sense that she fit the script. "God, you fuck. You are *just* as unoriginal. You settled for the same cookie-cutter life." He sighed and shook his head, trying to shake away the realization, not wanting it to settle and become true.

It was true though. She'd caught his eye because she was stereotypically pretty, she was easy to date because she followed all the rules, and she made a wonderful wife because she continued to follow the rules. But it left him wanting more, and that desire was what led him to Flora.

Flora was easy too, but she was easy in a different way. She was easy because she saw his soul, because she understood him and challenged him. He felt like a better person when he left Flora, more solid, more himself. He couldn't say that he felt the same about his time with Jill. He didn't need to think about things with her because it was all scripted. Their interactions mimicked the ones you saw take place between every happy couple in a movie.

And, like those on-screen interactions, their relationship lacked depth. He and Jill did not *connect* like he connected with Flora. *Because it's unoriginal,* he thought. *There's nothing interesting or exciting, nothing new. Everyone knows the story, so there's nothing to explore. It's the standard lie that most couples spend their lives in.*

His reverie was interrupted when he realized he'd almost missed the turn into her parking lot.

"You've been brooding," she said as she opened the door and pulled him in. "Come tell me about it while we're naked in bed." Flora moved behind him, putting her hands under his shirt, moving them from his waist to his chest as his nipples got hard. He let her slip his shirt over his head and turned to kiss her, moving the straps of her dress off her shoulders so it fell away when she leaned back for air, exposing her

45

small, dark breasts and broad shoulders. "I love you brooding," she said as they fell into her bed.

***

The James's 10th anniversary dinner was scheduled for eight p.m. at one of the best restaurants in town. He'd picked it because it was French cuisine. Thinking about their honeymoon had reminded him he'd wanted to try this place, and even though it was short notice, he was able to get a reservation through his connections at work. The kids were having a sleepover down the street. Jill's friend had volunteered to keep them so she and Rupert could stay out as late as they wanted. "Or stay up and be as loud as we want," Rupert had added with a playful wink when Jill shared the plan.

"Oh, you're terrible, honey." She pretended to be annoyed.

"What do you think?" He looked up to see Jill walking down the stairs.

"Incredible. You look stunning." He meant every word. She did look stunning. She had picked a dress that was black satin, not her normal choice because the fabric clung to her curves. With the thin spaghetti straps and a thigh slit that was just a little too high, she looked nothing like the Vanilla Queen at this moment. "Wow." He drew in a breath. "Part of me just wants to stay home."

"Oh, come on. I'm all dolled up. We *have* to go out!" she insisted. "I want my nice dinner *and* some champagne too. Please, honey?" She adopted her playful, childish tone.

"Of course," he conceded. "How could I say no to you? And, how could I deny the other diners this view?" He held up her arm and twirled her around. "Let's go make everyone else jealous!" He ushered her out to the limousine he had rented for the evening.

In the back seat, she sat close and put her head on his chest. "Honey, can you believe it's been ten years? Ten years. I feel like it has flown by."

"I know, Jill, it has gone by fast. Ten years married, but almost fifteen together, you know."

She smiled one of her wide "he loves me" smiles when he said this, activating his guilt. "You did make me wait for a long time before you proposed." She poked him in the rib jokingly. "You're lucky I'm a patient gal." He cringed. He hated when she used expressions like "dolled up" and "gal" because they were so… old-fashioned and silly. Unoriginal *and* out-of-date.

Rupert, you're an asshole, he told himself. *Enjoy this evening. You have a date with a wonderful woman who loves you, looks phenomenal, and is your wife. What more could you ask for?* But he knew what more he could ask for, although in some ways his hands were tied.

"You OK, hon? You just got tense." Jill sat up to look him in the face. "I was just joking."

47

"I'm fine, Jill. Give me a kiss." He pulled her face gently toward his and kissed her lightly on the mouth. He continued kissing her, moving his lips to her cheek, down her neck, brushing her hair out of the way to kiss her clavicle and continued to the top of her dress, near her breast.

"Ooh, you're making me wet," she cooed. "You better stop." She pulled away a bit but moved to sit straddling his lap, continuing to let him kiss her. He moved his fingers underneath her dress, feeling her warm and wet. "Don't stop," she said breathlessly, and he gently moved his index finger over her clit a few times before inserting it inside her. He could feel her tense with pleasure, and she kissed him harder.

The limo pulled up in front of the restaurant just then, stopping the momentum. She was not one for public displays of affection and the lack of movement made her self-conscious that the driver would see what they were doing.

"Jill, he'll wait." Rupert tried to keep her there, but her mind was already somewhere else.

She straightened her dress and checked her hair in the reflection on the window. "OK, I'm ready for dinner." She smiled, giving him a quick kiss on the lips.

He pasted on a smile in return but found himself disappointed. Someone who wasn't so vanilla would have fucked him in the car. And in fact, she had.

Chapter 5

Rupert turned from the clock to stare at the ceiling. It was three thirty a.m. He tried for another fifteen minutes but knew there was no way that he would be rescued by sleep. Rather than toss and turn, potentially waking Jill up, he rolled out of the warmth to head to his study.

Padding downstairs in his leather slippers and soft housecoat, he let the comfort envelop him. He and Jill had worked together to select the décor and furniture for each room, so they were all a mesh of their styles. Her preference for the mundane was punctuated by his selection of unusual or antique pieces, but somehow it worked.

The exception was his study, a room of his own making. He had opted for a traditional dark wood and leather theme. It *was* traditional and therefore unoriginal, but he'd always wanted a study with a mahogany desk and regal punched leather chair. The space was framed by the expected built-in bookshelves, full of the volumes he'd collected over the years.

A few belonged to Jill, but she wasn't a reader. At least not in a respectable kind of way. She was more the Oprah book club type, whereas he preferred *literature*. Sometimes, a book of hers would make its way onto one of his shelves. Upon discovering the intrusion, he'd move it back to the living room or often relocate it to the trash. It was compulsive, he couldn't just leave them be. Since no one but the two of them entered the room, and her very infrequently at that, it wasn't as if he needed to worry that he'd be judged by the dime store novels polluting his collection. Maybe it was just that he wanted a space all his own.

Which he did have since Jill rarely infringed. When she wanted to talk or question him, she'd open the door only part-way, never more than half, to speak softly, voice only half-penetrating as well. He really could have hidden anything in there, she'd never have known. Was she even curious? Was his mother ever curious?

He'd just settled in his chair with a hot cup of tea when the phone rang. "What the…" He grabbed it quickly to prevent the noise from rousing anyone else. "Hello?" he said quizzically. It was 4.15 a.m.

"May I speak to Rupert James, please?"

"This is he. What is it?" he asked, though his consciousness was almost done tracing the call to the hospital as he registered the buzz of activity on the other end.

"Mr. James, this is Margaret Yardley. I'm an RN at Memorial Hospital. I'm calling to let you know that your father has regained consciousness. We are not sure for how long, so if you want to speak to him, I would suggest heading down here as soon as possible."

"Ms. Yardley, thank you for your call. As I'm sure you know, I'm out of state and have no desire to speak to *that man* you have there. You may want to call my sister, Greta Gabler. She's local. Do you have her number?"

"Yes, sir, I do. I will give her a call. Thank you." She hung up abruptly.

She must think I'm a terrible person. And speaking of terrible, Rupert wondered if she knew who her patient, Rupert Nathanial James I, really was. Would it change the way she treated him? It would certainly influence him if *he* was in her position. *I wonder what Greta will do,* he thought next. He figured he'd wait a few minutes, then call her on her cell to see what she'd decided.

"Morning, bro," she said sleepily when she picked up the call. "So, they called you too?"

"Yes, I'm the decision-maker, so I guess I'm the first contact. I told her I had no desire to speak to 'that man' and she promptly ended the call. Do you think she knows who he is?"

"Of course, she does, bro. But nurses can't let that affect them. They're trained professionals and all that." She said it with more confidence than she probably felt. "Anyway, I'm on my way over there."

"What are you going to say?"

"Nothing. I have nothing else to say to him. I just want to see if he's interested in talking. Maybe apologizing or something before he leaves this mortal coil and all."

"Well, while you're there, see if you can get him to sign a DNR." He was tired of being in the hot seat. "It's the least he can do, the asshole."

"Sure, I'll see. But you know if I don't bring it up in the right way, he'll refuse to do it just out of spite." She was right. Rupert could hear the old man sneering, "Are you kids trying to finish me off?"

"Yeah, of course he will. How's Mom doing?" Rupert transitioned from one parent to the next as usual. "Is she aware of what's happening?"

"You mean did she get a call that he's awake? No, she doesn't know, and I don't think she'd care. She can't deal with much more after all that's happened the last two years. I'm sure she heard me get up, so I'll have a talk with her when I get back to the house. Make sure she's OK and all." Mary had moved in with Greta and her husband permanently after she was released from the hospital. They had sold the old house and most of her things. Greta's husband, who was more kind and gracious than any of the James men, had set up a whole wing of the house for their mother, even converting one room to a kitchenette so she could do what she wanted without feeling like she was always sharing space with the two of them.

"Thanks, Greta." Rupert was grateful for all she'd done to help their mother. "I know she's grateful too."

"Yeah, whatever, bro. I don't have time for your guilt. Talk to you later, OK?"

"DNR," he repeated. Then, "Love ya!" and quickly hung up. A moment later, his phone pinged with a text – the middle finger emoji. He laughed.

Later that day, Greta called to share that their father had in fact signed a DNR, relieving Rupert of at least one of his burdens.

"So, they were really able to get someone at the hospital to verify that he was of sound mind and legally competent? Impressive," Rupert quipped.

"He said he wanted to die," Greta told him. "He said he wished they could just kill him now. I had to tell him to keep that shit quiet in order to sign. A big part of me was in agreement. And not because I hate him, it's honestly because seeing him suffer is so hard. I fucking wish it wasn't, I feel like it shouldn't be, like I shouldn't care after all he did, but I do." She sighed.

"I hear ya, Greta. I was discussing the same thing just the other day. I'll tell you what my friend told me: 'Don't be upset at evidence that you are a good person.'"

"Are you passing on advice from your *mistress*?" she hissed the last word in a hushed tone, playing with him.

"How'd you know that was Flora?"

"Seriously?" she scoffed. "How about because the only insightful, intelligent things you share with me are from her? I mean, Jill's great and all but she doesn't have that level of depth."

"Don't insult her." He tensed as he became reflexively defensive.

"Jeez, bro. Chill out, sorry. I didn't mean anything by it. You know what I mean."

"Yeah, I'm sorry." He paused. "I think I feel bad about the whole thing, the affair, so I'm oddly protective of her. Isn't that fucked up? I won't stop it but I'm protective of her. I've got real problems."

"Yeah, you're a selfish prick, but hey, no one's perfect." She laughed. "Some are just worse than others." Her words reminded him of the conversation he'd had with his father and they didn't sit well.

"I gotta go. Call me if something changes."

"Sure thing." And they hung up.

***

The next day, The First transitioned to a new plane of existence. Greta called, she was there when it happened. It was better than hearing it from the hospital staff, he supposed. "And apparently, he has a standing agreement to donate his body to science or something, so we'll get the cremated remains whenever they are done dissecting him or whatever the fuck they do. Creepy, huh?"

"Yeah, creepy. OK, well, I got to get some work done. Thanks, Greta. I'm glad to be able to start putting this behind us. Talk soon. Love ya!"

He knew he should have asked her how she was, he could hear the desire to talk in her voice. That's what made him end so abruptly, he was just tired of discussing emotions. Turning back to his computer, he tried to begin (again) on the project he'd been attempting to knock out the last few days. The recent events had left him well beyond a little distracted.

A few minutes later, he heard a knock on the door and the creak as Jill opened to ask, "Everything OK? I thought I heard you talking to Greta."

He was irritated, wanting to get back to work. "Yes, fine. He died, that's all."

"Oh honey, I'm so sorry." He could tell she wanted to help, wanted him to want her help.

It made him angry. *Doesn't she know I'm not upset?* "Jill, I really need to get some work done. Can we talk later?" he snapped, hurting her feelings, knowing he was an asshole yet still convincing himself she deserved it for intruding.

"Yes, sure, honey. I'll keep the kids away too. Let me know if you need anything." She quietly closed the door and slunk away.

God, I am an asshole. How can I defend her to Greta and then treat her like this? What is wrong with me? He felt the tension build, radiating from his forehead around his skull. Rubbing his temples, he tried a soothing mantra to relax so he could get this project finished.

Turning back to the computer after a few minutes as his muscles relaxed, he boomeranged back as the phone rang. "Fuck!" he hollered, louder than intended. *God, please don't let that summon Jill,* he thought. *I'll yell at her too.* "Hello," he said angrily as he answered, not looking at the caller ID.

"Is this Rupert James?" a quiet voice asked, perhaps put off by his tone. *God, how many times has that been the first question on a phone call these days,* he thought. *What is the hospital calling about now?*

"This is. What'd you need?"

"Hi, Mr. James. I'm, I'm sorry to bother you, but I need to, I need to talk to you. You see, well you see, I think, I think my father, my father just d-died. My father…" She trailed off.

He waited to see if she would continue. "Yes…" he prompted, annoyed at the delay.

"You see, I think that my father… well, that my father was, was your father."

"I'm sorry, what?" He was incredulous; it took a few moments to process. "*Your* father was *my* father? Rupert Nathaniel James? I don't understand. I have a sister and a brother, *had* a brother. That's it. Who *are* you?" The words were coming out quickly, as he spoke the thoughts coming to mind.

"I'm sorry." He could hear the sob in her voice. "This is really, it's just really h-hard. I think, I think that you might be, that you might be my, m-my half-brother. That your fa-fa-father was my father too."

"Ma'am, I don't know what kind of quack you are or what your game is, but I really don't need this shit right now." His heart was racing, all effects of the mantra banished. *Just hang up,* he told himself.

"Mr. James, I know. I'm sorry, I'm very sorry. It's, it's just that my mother, she just told me yesterday that the man she saw on TV, the man in trouble for all that child porn, that he was my father. She said they had an affair around the time I was conceived and the man who raised me, the man I called 'Dad' was not my real father. I was going to see if I could visit him in the hospital, but when I went this morning, they told me he was dead. I was given your c-contact number."

"OK, lady." He'd had enough. "I can't deal with this right now. Give me your name and number and I'll call you back in a couple of days. Can you wait that long?" He wrote down her number and promised to call her back by the end of the week.

"I'm really sorry," she sobbed. "I know that this, t-this is difficult for you. But please, p-please try to imagine, well, it's hard for me too. I mean, I, I believed that the man who raised me was my father. I find out this, this isn't true, which is hard enough, but on top, on top of that, I find out that my *real* father might be some disgusting convict." He could hear her turn from sad to angry as she spat out those last words with derision.

Rupert reacted on impulse. "You didn't know him; you have no right to judge!"

"I'm sorry. You're right, I'm sorry." She placated. "I spoke harshly. I'm upset."

He was sure that she was softening her position in response to his anger and the desire to increase the odds that he would in fact call her back. "But, are you really defending him?"

"Maybe." He'd rather not think about that right now. "I've got to go. I'll be in touch."

Moving his eyes from the phone to his computer, and realizing there was little chance he'd get his work done now, he moved them back and dialed his mom. "Mom, it's Rupert. Do you have some time to talk?" He knew she did, she would always make time to help her kids, but he wanted to show that he respected her by asking.

"Of course, Pip, what's up?" she asked, using the term of endearment she'd anointed him with in childhood after they'd read *Great Expectations* together. "I'm not sure why, but you remind me of Pip," she'd said. "And it's a fun name."

"Mom, please," he said, feigning irritation. He was over getting upset about the nickname. Initially, he found it insulting, then embarrassing as he got older, and finally, he just appreciated it as evidence that he had a loving mother. But, he knew she liked the playful teasing, so he'd pretend to be bothered.

He told her about the woman who had called and her claims against The First. "Do you think it could be true?" he ended and waited for her to share.

"Pip, no, God no. For all your father's faults, that was not one of them. I can tell you with absolute certainty that he never cheated on me. He never would have even *thought* of doing that. His morals might have been skewed, but he wasn't *that* kind of man. He wouldn't do that to me."

As she said it, the way she said it, his heart dropped because he knew that, for her, cheating on your spouse was worse than what his father had done. He felt as if he'd been punched in the stomach, his breath caught. Was it possible? Was it possible that if she knew, his mother could think that *he* was worse than his father? How could it be? Was it really worse to have an affair?

He felt sick and needed to move off this topic. She was still talking, but he interrupted her. "OK, Mom, I'll call her back, see if I can find out more info and what her motives might be. But, it seemed like maybe she just wanted to know. Can I ask you something else?" He was hesitant because he'd never asked her about it before.

"Son…" she asked, drawing him out after the pause lingered.

"How did you not know something was wrong with Dad? How could you not know? I'm not, I'm not blaming you, I'm just curious."

She sighed. "Pip, I loved your father and I loved you kids. Love, well, it makes it so you don't even look for what might be going on. Plus, I was so busy with you all, the house, and helping your father. I know, I know I was just a stay-at-home mom, but I was *so busy*. Always preoccupied with something, I guess I just didn't see because I didn't know there was something to see. I wasn't looking." She sighed again, sadly.

Fuck, he thought as she talked. *That'd be Jill's excuse too. She is so busy with the kids and taking care of me and she* loves *me. She's not even looking, because I bet if she did, she'd know that something was wrong. Careful as I am with Flora, there are always signs. Were there signs with Dad too then?* he wondered with a tinge of regret.

She continued when he didn't say anything. "I guess maybe I should have been suspicious, maybe when your father moved into the apartment, but then I was hurt. I was so focused on being a victim that I was looking in, not out. I wish I was more aware, maybe I would have seen something, caught something. Maybe I could have helped him, so it didn't get to this point."

"Mom, no." He had to stop her from going down this path. "I'm not going to let you do this. You are not to blame for what happened to him. You wouldn't have been able to stop him, even if you knew. And imagine how much harder this would have been to take if it came out when we were kids. If it came out when you were still in love with him? Don't go there."

"Sure, sweetie." She was happy to let it go. "I just know he would never cheat," she said, transitioning back to the original topic. It was easier for her to defend his moral character than focus on his failings because she *had* loved him, and probably still did.

"OK, thanks, Mom. Sorry to bring stuff up. I'll let you know what else I find out. Have a great day. I've got to get back to Jill and the kids. I've been pretty absent the last couple of days. Love you."

"Love you too, Pip. Take care."

Chapter 6

"Can you believe her?" He was still upset by his conversation with his mother a few days earlier. "It's like she would have found more moral failing in The First if he had cheated on her than in what he did. I mean, one behavior is *criminal*, the other one isn't. Shouldn't that tell her something?"

He was in bed with Flora. She liked to talk after they made love, as they lay there naked. "You can't hide things as well when you're naked. Your body is honest and so your mind will be more honest too," she told him that once, soon after they'd met. "Let's always have serious conversations naked." He could see no reason to protest.

"Well," Flora started slowly, like she always did when she was thinking about how to formulate her response. "The first thing I would ask you is what difference does it make if one behavior is criminal and the other isn't? *And*, they were both criminal at some point. *And*, I'd wager a guess that your father's behavior wasn't criminal at some point in the past. In fact, we know it wasn't."

"Unbelievable, you take the wind out of my sails every time I try to present a strong argument. I must be so easy for you." He wasn't upset, but it was true.

He was lying on his back, looking at the ceiling, so he turned up on his elbow to look at her and kiss her chest as he spoke.

"I guess it was just an easy place to start," he continued. "Although I don't think that society should dictate your morals, I do think that actions that carry criminal penalties are penalized by law because they are bad, and potentially worse than those that aren't penalized… but you're right. It's not a good reason. It's the way a child would reason, that something is wrong because a rule says it's so."

"Sure, you're right. That's the easy place to start. Now, the hard part." She grabbed his semi-erect penis as she said this. "We need to talk a little more, I guess." She smirked.

"Flora, fuck, stop it. That's not fair."

"Remember what I said about honesty? Your naked body has a hard time lying." She smiled and turned to move him back on his back, sitting up to straddle him so he could see her curves, her stomach, and feel her wetness on his skin. "But, back to the hard part. Which is, why are you really so bothered by this?"

"I know why, and I don't want to have to say it. But, you're right, I need to say it." He sighed and stumbled through the door he'd rather keep closed. "It bothers me because it makes me think that she would think I was a worse person than my father. She'd judge me more harshly than she judged him. And I couldn't take it. He's despicable, what he did, and to do it for so long. All the lying, the deceit, happening right in front of us, with a family and kids of his own. And I'm just…" He trailed off.

"You're just what?" She couldn't help but probe what he tried to avoid. "You're just what?" She leaned back to stretch and moved her hips to spread her wetness over him as she asked the question, as if she was taunting him.

"God, you're evil," he said, feeling himself getting harder. "You know, you're part of the reason that I'm in this position. How could any man resist you? You don't play fair."

"So, you're just… a victim?" she asked, sliding her body down toward his feet and leaning forward so she could kiss his thigh as she straddled his calf.

"Yes." He laughed. "I'm clearly a victim, in the clutches of a gorgeous siren. What else can I do?"

He let himself take in the pleasure of her lips on his skin a bit more before he continued. "But seriously, I guess I'm just in a quandary because I want to feel like I'm a better person than The First, but my mother, and all this other shit that has been happening, it's all, well, it's all just making me feel like I'm not."

"And, so what are you going to do about it?" she asked forcefully, but not unkindly. "End the affair? How unoriginal would it be to make your decisions based on what your mother wants?"

"Fuck, I don't know. I do feel like a child though. I'm torn between what I want and what I should do.

If you'd just let me run away with you, all my problems would be solved." He looked at her pleadingly.

"Ha." She laughed, pulling back from her kissing. "You know how I feel about that, love."

He did. She'd explained her position to him the first day they'd met, which was the first day they'd made love, probably the first day he had ever truly made love.

He'd seen Flora sitting alone at a table in a coffee shop he visited on occasion, to get away from the office when he was there for more than a few hours. She'd been in a couple of times, and each time she'd caught his eye. He sensed that she was something special, deep, intense, and fiery. Something about the way she sat, the way she held herself told him that she was nothing like vanilla.

On a whim, one day he got his order and just sat down at her table, not saying a word. She'd looked up slowly and their eyes caught. He asked her later what made her interested in him, and she mentioned the sparkle of mischief in his eye at that moment. "Something made me wonder what was behind those eyes," she'd told him. "You seemed different. And you're more than I expected. I'm rarely surprised by people, but you were, you are, surprising."

After a little banter at the table, he learned she was a freelance graphic designer. "Oh, perfect," he told her. "I'm in need of a consultation. Do you work here or do you have an office somewhere we can retire to?"

"One better," she countered, "I work from home. And, it's just around the corner. Come, I'll show you." She packed up her things and they headed to her apartment. It was then that she gave him the spiel:

"Listen, I can see that you're married and honestly, I don't care. What I do care about though is that you don't attempt to leave her for me. I don't want that."

"We just met." He started to protest, but she held up her finger to stop him.

"Please let me finish." He nodded compliantly as she continued. "You cannot leave her for me. I won't have it. I'll leave you in return. You have kids with her?" He nodded again.

"Exactly. I don't want kids, I don't want a relationship that involves them. If you leave her, you will still have the kids and I'm not interested in making a family with someone else's offspring. If you think I'm selfish, fine. Just know that this is where I stand."

At the time, he wasn't sure what to make of it, so he set it aside. After she said her piece, they talked for a while, topics he could never discuss with Jill, that never came up when he was with her. Flora had depth and her own perspective, she was a challenge. *This is what I have been missing,* he thought as his love started to blossom. Their conversation continued as they moved from her couch to the bed and they enjoyed what he considered to be some of the best sex he'd experienced.

"I don't discuss that," she'd told him when he asked for her opinion. "There's no value in it. You'll ask me to make comparisons and I can't lie, so why do that? If you ask me if I like something, I'll tell you and please do the same for me. But don't ask me questions like, 'How was it?' I won't answer."

He loved how she was so direct, in some ways complicated and in other ways completely uncomplicated, like those finger handcuffs. But more... more magical. Who uses that description? It seemed an exaggeration, but it was accurate to how he felt. And her smell, God, she was intoxicating. The way her perfume mixed with her natural scent, enveloping him was a sensual invitation. He never tired of it, loved the way it lingered on his skin when he left her.

"I know," he said, coming back to the conversation at hand. "I wonder sometimes, what would have happened if I didn't have the kids."

"Love, it wouldn't make a difference, honestly." He sunk back as if he'd been stung. "Let me explain," she continued, wanting to soothe the hurt.

"We work because we have lives outside of this relationship. I think that most people need more than one person to meet their needs. Our needs are varied *and* variable. It's almost impossible to find just one person to give you all that you need. I bet that you get certain things from Jill that you appreciate that you'd never be able to get from me. This," she said, gesturing to the two of them, "this works because it's not the only thing we have. Kids or no kids, this is just one piece in the puzzle."

"Then you're saying that cheating isn't a bad thing, dove. It's normal and almost... necessary."

"That's my opinion. But I don't consider it cheating either. I just consider it another relationship in the midst of many. Cheating is a term that only applies when you have the belief that there is room for only one relationship."

"But everyone has more than one relationship."

"Yes, of course. And, I would argue that because of that, everyone cheats." She used air quotes on the last word. "Everyone has intimacies outside of their primary relationship, marriage or no marriage. While not everyone is sexually unfaithful, everyone is, in some sense, at minimum emotionally unfaithful."

She paused and played with his chest hair for a bit before continuing, giving him time to think. "I mean, even if you weren't doing this with me, you can still admit that there are things that you share with others that you'd never share with Jill."

"Of course, I have a different kind of relationship with her. Greta knows all kinds of things about me that Jill doesn't know. We talk about different things because she is different."

"But, that's exactly my point. Different people necessarily have different relationships. And we accept that. Everyone has just decided that there needs to be one romantic one, one special relationship that is built on sharing and trust, different from the rest, which is silly. Every relationship is built on sharing and trust, but you should only share to the extent that it's functional."

"I feel like you are just trying to excuse our behavior, dove. I mean, shouldn't you be looking for one person who *can* meet all your needs, so you don't need the extras and you don't need the lying?"

"Possibly, I'm not saying it *can't* be a goal. But what I am saying is that I don't think it's a goal you'd ever be able to achieve. That *one person* doesn't exist, not for anyone. Anyone who thinks they've found that person is lying to themselves. Even the closest marriages have secrets, of that I have no doubt."

"So, you're saying that lying is OK. It's necessary."

"Yes." She laughed. "That's how I started, love. I think that lying has its place in every relationship. I think that seeking truth at all costs is never good."

She sighed. "People try to pick rules to live by, black and white, because they can't handle the gray. Most people can't handle the gray. Rules make it easier, you don't have to think. But you and I, we live in the gray. We don't want things to be easy at the expense of experience."

"But." He paused, catching himself so he could respond thoughtfully. "I feel like you are now arguing for truth, dove. That the gray is truer than the black and white. That the rules make the lies, but the gray is truth."

"Yes, I guess you're right. Aren't you the clever one now?" She kissed him with a smile. "Challenging me, ha. I love it!"

He felt thrilled at her words. She was always the one that challenged; he was learning from her. "In a sense," she continued, "I'm arguing that we need to be true to our nature, not true to some set of rules that have been constructed to make people feel safe and secure. Opening up the possibility for other relationships opens up the possibility that your friend, partner, spouse, or whoever might find someone who they fit with better, who meets their needs more effectively, and that's scary. It's scary because it leaves you vulnerable. But, that vulnerability is important, because it's the only way that you can find out who you really are."

"Yes," he contemplated his agreement. "I guess you're right. I wouldn't want to tell Jill about you, even if there was no sex involved because she would be jealous. She'd see that we had a connection that the two of us didn't. But" – he paused as he approached a troubling thought – "who do you think is meeting her other needs? Lord knows I can't be meeting most of them."

"Ha." She laughed. "Weren't you *listening* to me? Who cares?" She threw her hands up in the air. "Or more realistically, what good would it do for you to know? Just like you see the value in lying to her about us, there is value in you not knowing everything about her and her relationships. What's good for the goose and all."

Yes, he thought as he turned to kiss her, *she is right. Lying is the only way for me to keep both, to have both her and Jill in my life.* Live in the gray… but perhaps this was what his father had thought. How he had justified his actions. He shuddered a bit, and not wanting to walk down that rocky path, he returned his attention to Flora and made it his goal to help her climax once more before he left.

Chapter 7

"What a bitch!" Greta was upset about the claims that their father had had an illegitimate child.

"Who's a bitch, Greta?" Rupert wasn't sure if she meant the mother or the daughter.

"This Lara woman. What does she want?"

"Honestly, Greta, I kind of felt the same way at first too, but now, well, now I kind of feel bad for her. I mean, she doesn't know who her father is. Why is she a bitch because of what her mother told her? What would you do in her situation?"

"Fine, then her mother's a bitch. She shouldn't have lied to her her whole life." Greta laughed a bit. "Listen, I'm hot, so someone needs to be a bitch here. I got to get this wrath out."

"Agreed, sis. So, I'd say the mom is the bitch then. I can't imagine lying to my kids like that their whole lives."

At this, Greta cleared her throat loudly. "Okay, pot."

"Come on, Greta. You're just like Mom. I know that having an affair isn't right, but it's not the same thing. Some lies are worse. I'm lying to the kids to protect them. There are some things that they don't need to know."

"True, but maybe the mother thought that she was protecting her daughter too. That her lie was necessary." She paused. "Fuck you, Rupert. Now you have me defending the bitch!" She said this last part with a laugh.

"You know not to test me," he replied playfully. "You walked right into my trap." The jest allowed them to move away from the topic that was making him feel increasingly unsettled. "Anyway, I'm going to get the test taken care of tomorrow, so we'll know one way or the other soon."

"K, keep me posted. Later, bro!"

***

A few days later, Rupert got a call from Lara, and she was crying. "He's not my father," she said through sobs.

"I'm sorry, I'm not sure what to say, Lara." Rupert felt bad for her, but he wasn't sure he wanted to be the one responsible for dealing with her baggage, especially since they barely knew each other. "I guess I'd tell you that maybe you should be happy. I mean, if he was then you'd have a disgusting convict for a father." He remembered her words from their earlier conversation. "I told you, my mom was confident he'd never cheated."

"Yeah, right. But, it's easy for someone who wants something to be true to insist that it's true. No disrespect to your mother, but you know what I mean."

"I do," he said. "I actually had a similar conversation with her about just that sentiment. What are you going to do now?"

She started crying again. "I'm sorry." For someone he'd just met, this woman had probably apologized to him more than anyone else in his life. "I'm just feeling very vulnerable. I mean, I'm back to not having a father again."

"What do you mean?" Rupert was incredulous. "You have a father. What about the man who raised you? Did you not get along?"

"Oh no. No, we had a great relationship. He was wonderful, always so supportive. Really unconditionally supportive, he was wonderful. But, he's dead. He died a few years ago, after a rough battle with ALS. It was awful to watch this vibrant man become so confined. My parents moved to Oregon, to participate in their physician-assisted death program and for that I was thankful."

Rupert felt compelled to move her past this tragedy. "Then you had a father, Lara. I'm not sure why you are so concerned." He felt his curiosity rising. "Why is it so important to find your biological father?"

"It's hard to explain... I'm not sure I really know why, to be honest. I've been thinking about that question a lot lately, trying to figure it out. I guess maybe part of it is that I miss Dad. I don't know, maybe I'm seeking the biological version because I want to replace the one I lost. I don't know. Does that make any sense?"

"Sure, it does. It's hard. It's hard to get over any good relationship that ends, especially when you weren't ready or didn't want it to. It's like how the easiest way to get over a break-up is to find a new partner. But, you have to be careful about that because you might not give yourself the time to process the loss." Rupert stopped himself as he began to sound trite. *Jeez, who am I to be giving advice anyway,* he thought.

"Yes, you're right. I don't know, but there's more too. I feel like I'm lost, ungrounded. The life I believed to be true all my life was really a lie. It makes you start to question things. Maybe answering this question will help me feel less like nothing is real."

"Interesting," Rupert pondered. "I'm trying to think about what you are saying in relation to my experience. I mean, the father *I* thought *I* had wasn't the man I believed him to be. That created some shit for me too, but I guess yours is worse because you really cared for yours. Mine was loving in a way" – it pained him to admit that, to say it out loud – "but we were never really close. He made us all feel like we never lived up to his standards. Aristocrats were what he wanted, and he saw us mostly as peasants, I think. My mom, on the other hand, now she saw us as kings and queen. Still does, I'd wager. How about you and your mother? What'd she say when you told her about the test?"

Lara started crying again.

"Lara, I'm sorry." Now it was Rupert's turn to apologize. "I didn't mean to upset you."

"It's OK," she sobbed. "It's just, she, she d-died two days ago. I don't know how I'll ever know who my father was now… and now I'm all alone." She broke down. Rupert felt trapped, anxious like a cornered mouse. How could he end the call now, with her in this state? *Change the subject, change the subject,* he chided.

"Lara, I'm really sorry. I can't imagine how difficult things are for you. Can I ask you something?" He was curious and hoping that if he got her talking, she would calm down enough to let him get off the phone without feeling too guilty.

"Sure, what is it?" He could hear her trying to control her breathing, to calm herself down.

"Well, I'm just wondering how you feel about your mother telling you. Would you have preferred that she just didn't say anything? Better that she died letting you believe that the man who raised you was your father? Or is it better that she told you the truth, even though you'll most likely never have an answer?"

"Well," she started slowly. "I guess it depends on your perspective and values, doesn't it? For me, the truth is always better than a lie. So, for that reason,

I'm glad she told me. It's going to be hard, to come to terms with the unknown, but that's better."

"Why?" Rupert challenged. He just didn't agree. "If she never said anything, you'd have gone on believing that the wonderful father you had *was* your father, and that would be that. What value is there in knowing what you know? You can't do anything about it so all it does is add unpleasantness to your life. The lie preserved a good thing, the truth created something that will always cause you pain. Why would you want that, just because it's the truth?"

"Because I value truth." She said it plainly, like there was nothing left to question. "And," she continued after a pause, "how do you know that the truth coming out is worse? Sure, right now I feel horrible and I may never find the answer to who my father is, but maybe the truth has opened up a whole new set of options for me that were never there before. You can't possibly know what the future has in store, and I want a future that is driven by truth."

"Hmm, interesting," he said, mulling over her words. "I'm not sure I agree with you though. I think there are times when a lie preserves something that is worth preserving. Especially if it covers up something that doesn't need to be known."

"Are you talking about your father?" It was Lara's turn to ask a tough question. "Do you think it would be better if his behavior was never discovered?"

"*Phhooo,*" he audibly sighed as he let out a deep breath. "That's a tough one, Lara. Part of me wishes that he was never caught, because then I could have gone on believing that he was the person I thought I knew. I mean, he wasn't great, but he didn't disgust me back then. And let me tell you, the burden of caring about someone who disgusts you is heavy. But does that mean that I excuse his behavior, that I think he didn't deserve to get caught and to be punished? No, I can't say that either. I guess you've stumped me. I've got a lot to think about here."

"Well, he wasn't my father, so I don't have any emotional attachment. I can say that it's better that he was caught because it can help make for a better future. There may be others who are deterred from doing the same thing because he got caught. In fact, his getting caught probably led to some other people getting discovered as well. But all that aside, I still maintain that it's better to know the truth."

"But *why*, Lara? Why is truth better?" He was really troubled by her certainty.

"Because, Rupert, think about it. A future built on a lie is someone else's creation. Whoever told the lie gets to shape your reality, that other person is in control of your world, and what you believe. Do you want someone else in control of your life? Not me, no, I'd rather let objectivity reign. Why should someone else get to determine my reality?"

Just then he heard his door creak. "Honey, dinner is ready. We're all at the table. Would you like me to bring your plate in here?" Jill was peering around the door, in case he made a non-audible response.

"No, sweetheart. I'll be right there. Thank you." He smiled, happy for her intrusion for once, her inadvertent rescue. "Lara." He returned to the phone. "I have to go. Thank you for the conversation. I'm sorry about your situation and I hope that you find the peace you need. Take care of yourself."

Rupert put down the phone slowly, then pushed back his chair and headed out to the dinner table.

"Daddy!" exclaimed Isabella, as if she was surprised to see him at the table. He tensed at the reminder that he had been so absent lately.

"What's for dinner, Chad?" he asked pleasantly, reaching down to kiss Isabella on the head before taking his seat at the head of the table, between Chad and Isabella and across from Jill's spot.

"Donno, ask Mommy." He was distracted tracing his matchbox cars along the edge of the table.

"I'll ask her!" Isabella was keen to be involved. "Mommy," she hollered toward the kitchen, "what're we eating?"

She came around the corner with the answer, something in a casserole dish. *Ugh, probably enchiladas,* Rupert thought. He was not a fan of her baked entrees and the aroma of Mexican spices accosted his nostrils. "Smells great!" he lied. "What do we say to Mommy for making a wonderful dinner?" he directed to the kids.

"Thank you, Mommy!" they chirped in unison. *They are great kids,* he thought and smiled. He worked to maintain his smile after taking his first bite under Jill's scrutiny.

"How is it?" she proffered.

"Delicious, Jill." He choked out the words as he choked down his meal.

Chapter 8

Because The First had decided to donate his remains to medical science, there was no body to lay out at a wake, nothing to bury. As a consequence, there would be no funeral plot, and no tombstone to mark the life that had expired.

But really, thought Rupert, would anyone have come if those things occurred? Would anyone have wanted to honor the life of the man who'd lived the life his father had?

Still, a few weeks after his departure, Rupert felt it was worth having a discussion with Greta to determine whether or not she thought a memorial service of some sort was in order. Maybe the two of them needed it to finally get some closure.

"Seriously, bro? Fuck no." Greta was not at all torn about what to do. "I don't want to be involved in anything of the sort. Memorial service? What would we be honoring? His ability to fool us all for so long? His accrual of a massive collection of smut? Fuck no." She repeated her final protest.

"Greta, yeah, I get it. I guess on some level I just want to feel like he's not all bad. I mean, what do you *do* with all the good memories?"

"Ha! Good memories? You're an ass. I think you might be falling victim to that death sanctification shit. You know, people are always talking about how someone's such a bastard, but then they die and all of sudden they were such a saint. Don't do it, especially not in this case. He may have fooled people into believing he was a good father once, but it was all a lie. *That's* what you should think about."

"I don't know that I totally agree with you, sis." He was thinking about the conversation he'd had with Flora the other day about shades of gray. "Isn't it possible that he was both? That he could be both, both a good father *and* do those things? I mean, people are complicated."

"Yes, bro. People are complicated. Write that down." She was dripping sarcasm. "Complicated," she scoffed, "but he wasn't good. I mean, I just wonder how he could judge us all the time, tell us that *we* needed to be better at living up to our *names* when he was scum. When he was doing all that shit. It's hard to come to terms with the fact that you learned your life lessons from a hypocrite. How do you know what's real?"

"Sure, fine. But do we ever know what's real? Why not just make your own decisions then? Who cares which lessons came from him and which from someone else? Why not just look at what you've learned, keep what you feel is helpful, and let go of the stuff that isn't? We're under no obligation to follow the rules he wanted us to."

"*Ugh,* I hate when you get all Flora on me. That woman really is trouble." He could hear that she was smiling though.

Although she'd never endorsed his affair, she was similar to Flora with respect to relationships. She had many friends, both male and female, outside of her marriage and some were very intimate. But, she'd never have an affair, not in the traditional sense. That was a betrayal of confidence in which she wouldn't participate. Still, she never once told Rupert that he shouldn't be having his. *Shades of gray, I guess,* he thought to himself.

"All right, so no ceremony it is. How's Mom?" He asked her his standard question to signal the end of their conversation. Greta gave him the standard two to three-sentence update, some version of "she was doing the best she could," and they said their goodbyes.

When he hung up, Rupert looked at his screen. He still had that project to finish. It had been trailing on for weeks. For some reason, he just couldn't muster up the energy and attention to get it finished.

Well, not "for some reason," he thought, *there is a reason. All this crap that's been happening lately.*

He sighed, pushing back his chair slightly, knowing that he wasn't going to be able to focus on his work. But what to do instead? Then it came to him – write an obituary. *Yes,* he thought, *I'll write an obituary for The First. I mean, if lies create reality, why not indulge?*

But where to start? It's not an easy thing to do, to write up a summation of someone else's life. Or maybe it's easy for some people, but it was difficult for Rupert. His mind traveled back to his brother's funeral. His mother had asked that he give the eulogy for Sebastian, but he wasn't the only one who spoke. And the contrast between his words and those of others still bothered him from time to time.

Sebastian had been emotional and moody, all his life. He was a petty and *particular* child, never easy in any situation. But, as his older brother, Rupert felt compelled to try to protect him. Especially against The First, who found Sebastian's sensitivity to be particularly troublesome. He'd often heard his father blaming Mary for the way Sebastian was: "You coddled him when he was young. I warned you about this. About treating him like a baby all the time."

Oh my God, the realization stung him again. *And I do the same thing to Jill. Fuck, I need to stop that. If my mother wasn't to blame for Sebastian turning out the way he did* – and Rupert didn't think she was – *then how could Jill be responsible for Chad?*

But, he moved back to his childhood, Sebastian was hard to protect, at least emotionally. He seemed to always find something troubling, something upsetting in everything that happened. Nowadays, people would say that he lacked resilience, but people didn't talk like that back then. Maybe if he'd tried less hard to protect him, Sebastian would have had to toughen up, and he would have been able to handle things better when he moved into adulthood. *Shit, there I go again, looking to place the blame. I'm no more at fault than my mother.* From guilt, to blame, to self-absolution. His emotional treadmill.

He had worked through these thoughts many times before, and contemplated them as he'd worked on the eulogy back then. Because Sebastian hadn't accomplished much – he'd been a history major in college, finished his degree without distinction, and held a series of meaningless mid-level jobs post-graduation – it was hard to think of what to say. The fucker was so unaccomplished, he didn't even leave a suicide note. At a loss, Rupert had decided to focus on his spirit, his soul, even though it was so cliché. Souls didn't even exist.

But, he thought about Lara, the lies *did* create reality. His speech was short, mentioning that Sebastian was a troubled soul, but he'd touched many lives. Then, he'd started to apologize. Going off script, he was speaking directly to that spirit which he had praised earlier, which didn't exist, couldn't hear the message that was too late, telling him that he was sorry. That he should have reached out more, that it was his responsibility to check in, to make sure that he was OK. Guilt then blame. Rupert knew he had checked out, given up his protector role when he'd gotten married and moved away. "I'm sorry, bro." That ended it.

The other speakers who followed were people who claimed to be Sebastian's friends, people whom

Rupert had no knowledge of but that his mother and Greta knew, at least in passing. There was a man he'd met in one of the many rehab groups he'd been marginally involved with. He talked about how Sebastian was in a better place and had found his peace. Rupert and Greta had caught each other's eyes and rolled them in unison at the cookie-cutter, meaningless words, viewing this individual as someone wanting to feel important by sharing these trite sentiments. Rupert tried to stop himself from judging, but of course, he'd failed.

There was also a woman, a former or current girlfriend. But he'd corrected himself, she had to be former since he was dead. Rupert knew very little about Sebastian's relationships. She talked only to Sebastian's ghost, her words professing her undying love for him, telling him that they would be together in the future and happy without the worries of the world. Afterward, Rupert asked Greta if he thought the two would be reunited sooner rather than later. "You're sick, bro," she scolded, but as he turned, she tapped his shoulder and mouthed, "Next week," with a somber, knowing nod.

He and Greta had always had that kind of connection, to share with dark humor their socially inappropriate commentary. She was definitely a relationship that he needed, and he was thankful for it. *And, at least with her,* he thought, circling back, connecting conversations, *I don't need to lie to Jill about it.*

So, what to say of his father's life? What would he have said had he died without all his crimes coming to light? Now *there* was an interesting prospect. What reality would that ongoing lie have sustained?

Mom would have asked me to give the eulogy, he was sure. So, let's see, what would I have said?

He started to type: "Ladies and gentlemen, we are gathered here today to honor the life of Rupert Nathaniel James, I. I want to thank you all for coming, and I know he would be heartened to see you all here. Thank you also for your kindness and support to my mother and the rest of our family during this difficult time. My mother has asked me to say a few words in memoriam, on behalf of the family." It would have had to be formal, in keeping with his aristocratic aims.

"My father was a complicated man, but one who was focused on self-improvement. And, because this was his goal, he was focused on helping, or forcing (*huh, Greta – always room for a bit of levity*, he thought as he typed in the meager attempt at humor), those around him to orient themselves this way as well. 'Work to be a better version of yourself' was something he'd often say. He pushed us to do that, and I'd argue it helped Greta and me achieve some success."

Would I have included Sebastian? He paused his typing to think. *No, no. He didn't achieve any success.*

"He was strict but loving and did what he could to make time for the family, although I'm sure my mother would have liked it if he was around more. I remember the games he'd invent for us as kids. To me, they showed both his desire to have fun but also to teach. A way to share the lessons that were important to impart. A creative way to show that there are rules... and rewards. And that rewards follow when you follow the rules. Because, as we all know, he *was* one to follow the rules."

He stopped himself at the contradiction. *He was* always *reminding us to play by the rules, but look at his own* life, thought Rupert with exasperation. *He was the ultimate hypocrite. Ah, but then again, who isn't?* He leaned back with a sigh, feeling heavy with his own contradictions.

To be a better version of yourself, that required knowledge of who you were. Self-insight was invariably something that The First lacked. It had to be, Rupert thought; otherwise, how could he keep on doing what he was doing? He drooped again as a new idea settled in. Perhaps, *that* wasn't the worst of what he'd done. Was it possible that when it ended there, where he was when he got caught, he *was* a better version of his former self? That he'd done *worse* things in his past?

"God, I'd hate to think of who he was if that was the case." He said it aloud, almost compelled to express it, a sentiment too awful for him to keep in.

Just then, he heard the soft knock on his door as she peered in.

"You in the middle of something, hon? I thought I heard you talking."

"No, just wasting time because I can't focus on my project. What's up?" He turned toward her with a smile, all too happy to let himself be pulled away from where he was headed.

"Nothing really. I was just about to get lunch ready. Just checking if you wanted something to eat."

"Sure, I'll come out in a bit. Whatever you're whipping up for the kids or yourself is fine with me. Thanks for checking." Then he paused, wanting to test their connection but hesitant to learn the truth. "Wait a minute, Jill," he called her back as she turned to leave. "I want to ask you something."

"Sure." She peeked back around the door. "What's up?"

"Come here," he said, calling her over to where he sat, pushing his chair back from the desk so she could sit in his lap. "Sit with me."

"What's wrong?" she asked as she settled sideways and put her arms around his neck.

"No, nothing's wrong." *God,* he thought, *I must never talk to her unless it's to share bad news. I need to work on that.* "I was just writing an obituary, well I guess a eulogy, for my father. I was thinking about what I would have said if he had died before the arrest, died before anyone knew."

She was waiting for him to finish, to continue his thought or maybe for him to ask her to read it. Hesitant to speak, as if it would break the spell. But after a prolonged pause, she prompted, "Did you want me to read it? You said you wanted to ask me something?"

He drew in his breath. It was hard to proceed, hard to ask those questions that you really didn't want to know the answer to, something he'd been doing a lot lately. "No, well sure, you can read it if you want to. But what I wanted to ask was, what do you think of me? Do you think I'm a hypocrite, like, like he was?"

She pulled her head back so she could look him in the eyes, as if startled by the question, and using shared eye contact to emphasize her honesty. "Absolutely not. You are wonderful. You are a wonderful husband and a wonderful father. You're nothing like he was. All that other stuff aside, you know he never cared about your mother or you kids. He couldn't have, doing what he did. You're nothing like him. Is that what has been bothering you for so long?"

Her words made him cringe, because he knew then what was true, and it wasn't what she spoke. He was no different than his father, although maybe he was a better liar when it came to protecting the feelings of those he claimed to love. His father hurt his mother, she was lonely in their marriage. He hurt his kids in some ways, never letting them believe that they were good enough. But Rupert, Rupert burned with the realization that he was worse.

I'm hurting them by hiding reality. I'm creating their world, just like Lara argued, but I'm creating the world that I think they should have. Don't they all have a right to create their own world? We're no different, my father and I.

And it hurt him, to hear his father's words echoing back. Those words spoken in the jail visiting room. "Everyone is flawed, everyone hides things from the world. Everyone does things that they know are wrong."

So, what to do about it? he wondered. *I guess there is only one thing. We all make choices and I get to choose. What lies do I want to keep telling and how much truth do I want to share?*

As the family sat together eating lunch a few minutes later, the doorbell rang. He received the delivery, a box containing his father's ashes. It seemed much lighter than he'd expected.

Chapter 9

A scent hit his nose, but it was unexpected, creating both pleasure and alarm as he took it in. "What's that?" he asked, turning around to see that Jill had gotten into bed next to him.

"What, hon?" she asked lightly. "What's what? Did you hear something?"

"No, no. I just thought, I got startled," he stuttered, trying to regain his composure. "Are you wearing a new perfume?" he queried.

"Yes, you noticed." She said it with that silly, wide loving smile. "I was walking through the store and it caught my attention. For some reason, when I smelled it, it reminded me of you. Do you like it?"

"Mmm, let me see," he said, nuzzling his nose up to her neck and grabbing her waist to pull her close to him. "Intoxicating," he said, voice muffled in her breasts. And it was, it was Flora's perfume. The mix on Jill was almost equally pleasant, but he was disconcerted at the breach. The lies create the reality, the *realities*, and things kept running together these days.

He'd been thinking, pushing himself, working, working to make some of the choices he'd challenged himself to make after he'd written the eulogy, after

Jill's response to his question. They were getting ready to move; the family was headed to a new town. He needed a change and Jill was up for it. "Yes! Let's make our mark somewhere new," she'd gushed when he asked her opinion. It pleased him, her use of the word "our," her belief in their collective, their joint ability to make a mark. His challenge to appreciate her more was also working.

The tough conversations were the ones he had with Flora. She, in her characteristic fashion, had dealt with it in stride, as if unburdened by any emotional strain. "Listen, love," she said, lying naked on her stomach, looking over at him as he lay beside her. "I don't want to have some long, sad goodbye. When it's time to go, you'll just go. Until then, let's keep meeting. Let it end when it ends, don't force things."

"Sure," Rupert responded, staring up at the ceiling. He'd been struggling with this part the most. "Dove, I love you. But, as you've made plain, we can't be together."

She stopped him. "I've never said that. We can't be together in the conventional way that you've been taught to want. I don't want that, I don't want those things. I could have been with you, could be with you forever, but not with what you'd bring with you at this point. That's what I said."

It was important to her that he understood her true meaning. "I understand, I'm sorry to mischaracterize. I mean, I understand your position," he corrected himself, "but I don't understand your *view*. I think there's a fundamental difference in the way we're oriented."

"Possibly," she said slowly. "Can you elaborate?" Always fair, she wanted to make sure not to misunderstand him in return.

"Sure," he said with a small laugh. Sometimes, it was like speaking with an attorney, but there was always value in her probing. "I don't know that I agree with you completely about relationships. I think that every relationship involves sacrifices. Sometimes, I think that you use my kids as an excuse to avoid full commitment, as a way to prevent yourself from having to make a hard choice."

"Love, they're not an excuse. I know what I want, and it's not that. Are you saying you think I'm incapable of being fully committed to *one* person? And that I'd find an excuse with everyone to keep my distance, to keep things unconventional?"

"No, I'm not sure what I'm saying. I guess it's my ego, trying to convince myself of something. I don't know." He trailed off, trying to collect his thoughts.

"I don't *want* to feel that I have to be with one only person. I don't *want* to compromise," she asserted. "That doesn't mean I *can't* do it. You're the only person who I'm with, the only person who I have been with since I met you. So, in that sense, I'm committed. More committed than you are."

She paused and looked up to see his reaction. She didn't say it to hurt him, but she knew it would aggravate the wounds he harbored, this festering moral sore the affair had created. "That idea that relationships take compromise is something that arose because we've been taught to fit our feelings into a mold that they weren't made for. It's stifling. Relationships take compromise, fuck that."

"But" – he was ready to challenge her, as often happened when she took a strong position – "but, don't you think that *every* relationship you are in requires compromise? You can't be friends with someone, in any meaningful way, unless you sometimes put their desires above your own. In some respects, that's a compromise."

"We're talking about two different things though, love." This impasse was more than conversational, a neon "No Vacancy" sign that Rupert had ignored for too long. "You and everyone else, you talk about compromise as a virtue in relationships because it's hard. I don't see virtue in something just because it's hard. And, I don't think that real relationships *are* hard."

"You don't think it takes work to maintain a relationship?" He wanted to know more, to extract as much knowledge as possible before he closed the door for good.

"No, to me, relationships are like the tide, they fade in and out. Think about it, any of the really good relationships you've had, they have an ebb and flow. We are taught to seek a kind of permanence from others that's unnatural. Everything changes, people change, why should we expect relationships to be any different?"

"Sure, I see your point. But isn't a solid relationship one where the partners work to change together?"

"To me, a solid relationship is one where the partners work to help each other improve. To become better, together. Wouldn't you say that's what we do?"

"Yes!" he replied emphatically. "And that's why I wanted to be with you."

She sighed, and her sigh made it all so final. Fitting the last piece in a complex puzzle, that sense of accomplishment mixed with the disappointment of needing to dismantle and start over. "You *are* with me. The problem is that you need more than that."

She was right, he needed more, wanted more. He didn't mind that she challenged his view on the role of work in relationships. For him, it *was* a good thing, *he* valued it.

"Go back to her, move with her." Flora pushed him away lovingly. "She gives you more of what you need. Our chapter has been written, and so goes life. The chapters begin and end, but you turn the page and start anew. And so it goes. The cycle will continue, unless you decide to break it." She paused and looked him in the eye. "Don't break it, love," she insisted, leaning in for a passionate kiss.

***

As they settled into their new house, he and Jill went to work setting up the rooms as they had in the old house, with a mix of him and her. He found more pleasure in her contributions this time, wanting to see what she would discover and how he could match or add to it. "Isn't this fun?" she asked him with joy as they walked through a store, her wide smile present so frequently these days. "You'll have to stop it soon, or I'll want to move again to do this all over," she offered playfully as they worked on positioning their purchases in the living room.

He smiled back at her but didn't respond. His thoughts wandered to ponder his own reality. *She trusts me, I can't let her down,* he reminded himself. He'd thought about leaving her, not for Flora of course, but because he knew he'd treated her poorly. Maybe it's best if I let her go? He'd thought about telling her the truth, the truth about Flora and the affair, letting her make her choice, letting her construct her own reality rooted in truth, like Lara argued for. *Maybe it's best if she gets to make the decision?*

But in the end, he made a different choice, the choice to move away from temptation, to start anew. *She loves me and she trusts me, that's her reality,* he told himself. *Yes, I've helped to construct it but the construction is hers as well. Another joint project of our family. She sees me, a version of me that works, and I can try to be more like that. I don't want to just* seem *like that person, I want to* be *that person. That way, we can share the reality moving forward.*

And who knows what lies she's used to construct my *reality?* He thought about that often too, but he would catch himself before he wandered too far down that path. Better not to explore too deeply, lest he find something unpleasant. The lies construct reality, so why not let it be, let the tide bring what it may?

Jill walked over to a box, and unwrapped one of her favorite vases, setting it up on a shelf. She'd always preferred vases to flowers. She hated flowers because their beauty didn't last, there was nothing permanent in such a gift. "Is here OK, hon?"

"Sure, looks great," he lied. It was pastel; of course, it was, with two doves entwined with a laurel branch. A prized possession she had brought back from one of her weekend trips a year or so ago. Although Rupert didn't particularly care for it, he knew how much she liked it so he didn't mind it being prominently displayed. She'd never let him see the inscription on the bottom: *"Jill, my love, with you in my life, I am whole."*

Printed in the USA
CPSIA information can be obtained
at www.ICGtesting.com
LVHW040807040824
787206LV00004B/815